ANGEL ACADEMY

The Seven Keys

Joanne Wiess

ANGEL ACADEMY

The Seven Keys

Joanne Wiess

CITIOFBOOKS, INC.
3736 Eubank NE Suite A1
Albuquerque, NM 87111-3579
www.citiofbooks.com

Hotline: 1 (877) 389-2759
Fax: 1 (505) 930-7244

Ordering Information:

Quantity sales. Special discounts are available on quantity purchases by corporations, associations, and others. For details, contact the publisher at the address above.

Printed in the United States of America.

ISBN-13:   Softcover   979-8-89391-796-3
             eBook   979-8-89391-798-7
             Hardback   979-8-89391-797-0

Library of Congress Control Number: 2025914092

Contents

PREFACE ii
CHAPTER ONE 1
CHAPTER TWO 5
CHAPTER THREE 12
CHAPTER FOUR 19
CHAPTER FIVE 23
CHAPTER SIX 26
CHAPTER SEVEN 30
CHAPTER EIGHT 34
CHAPTER NINE 39
ABOUT THE AUTHOR 55

PREFACE

Intricately tiered roses bloom with jagged thorns on their stems.

Sharp, intimidating barbs protect the astoundingly complex flower.

Bristles guard the beauty.

The reality of the balance screams to be appreciated!

Let's highlight balance further by delving into the realm of angels.

There are three spheres of angels.

The first grouping is the Seraphim, Cherubim, and Thrones. They represent the burning zeal, constantly glorifying and praising.

The second encompasses Dominions, Virtues, and Powers that regulate the duties of the lesser angels and ensure cosmic order.

The third includes the angels closest to humanity - Principalities, Archangels, and Angels.

This tome is exclusively about angels and archangels.

Angels abide as pure beings of light.

Their very existence illuminates the non-earthly, abstract concepts of hope, faith, trust, and love.

They serve as messengers who aid in restoring the internal balance that should be present in each individual.

Inspiration and harmony are their hallmark.

Joy, peacefulness, and clarity are enhanced when they draw near.

Angels

- exist to lead back to the eternal source of perfect balance.
- are not assigned a sexual orientation or a visible body. If they manifest in the presence of humans, the human's expectations

dictate their form.

- never interfere with the choices of humans but rather offer a range of inspired possibilities when decisions need to be made.
- never insist; humans are free to follow their nudges or not.
- are constantly available to answer any call because they do not sleep.
- are not limited, they can respond to many inquiries at once.

The goal of the angels and archangels is to aid in the restoration of internal balance in the life of the human.

Angel Academy offers an arena for all angels to master the ways that humans assess their environment. This knowledge, collected as the seven keys of learning, enhances their ability to be helpful to humans seeking assistance.

Angel Academy: The Seven Keys

1. Introduction: Learning and the Angels
   I am coming, and I will live among you. Zechariah 1:10b
2. Sight and the Angels
   Suddenly, an angel appeared, and a light shone in the cell. Acts 12:7a
3. Hearing and the Angels
   The angel said to me in the dream, 'Jacob.' I answered, 'Here I am.' Genesis 31:11
4. Tasting and the Angels
   Then he lay down under the bush and fell asleep. All at once an angel touched him and said, "Get up and eat."   1 Kings 19:5
5. Smelling and the Angels
   There the angel appeared to him in flames of fire from within a bush. Exodus 3:2
6. Touching and the Angels
   There was a violent earthquake, for an angel came down from heaven and, going to the tomb, rolled back the stone, and sat on it. Matthew 28:2
7. Sensing and the Angels
   The angel said to him, "I am Gabriel. I stand in the presence of God, and I have been sent to speak to you and to tell you this good news. Luke 1:19
8. Contacting the Angels
   Angels speak to those who silence their minds long enough to hear. Proverb
9. NET Adventure Stories

(All quotes from New International Version Bible.)

CHAPTER ONE

I am coming and I will live among you.
Zechariah 1:10b

Learning and the Angels

Angel Academy is the center of learning for angels who interact with humans. Each angel needs to earn the seven keys of insight to "graduate" thus increasing the likelihood that encounters with earth dwellers will prove effective.

The story behind the founding of Angel Academy will highlight the need for the school.

Originally, the core of existence exhibited complete and total stability.

This balance is the zero-

- the perfect, endless embodying of the integrated essence of desire and manifestation.
- fluid and expanding.
- infinitely looping within the core.

This eternal flux is the balance.

It is in this state that the universe was birthed, so that the constancy continues in every emerging form.

Zero allowed the universe to burst into existence, hatching the cosmic egg, seeking to replicate itself in arrangements that are samples of the balanced core material.

This equilibrium naturally recognizes choice, which allowed the unbalanced an opening; giving rise to those who could lead to its restoration – angels and archangels.

Humanity exists on the planet Earth.

It does not need angels or archangels to validate its existence, but inherent sensory distractions invite humans to stray from the natural desire for balance.

Angels can lead humans back to internal harmony and offer quiet inspiration.

Angels do not need earth dwellers to be complete as beings, but the desire to manifest balance draws their attention.

Angels do not have senses, so helping humans was initially an uneasy task.

To effectively aid, angels sought lessons about human sight, sound, taste, hearing, and touch, which could enhance their reach into the realm of humanity.

A platform for absorbing these sensory concepts was developed into a school, founded to teach ways of relating to humans to increase impact.

Angel Academy was vested.

There are several tracks for angels at the academy.

Numbered assignments are as follows:

Archangels sport numbers from 000 to 999. This is the center of learning for encounters between the human realm and angels.

Support angels have numbers running from 1000-2999. They work to spark positive choices.

Guardian angels are 3000-3999 and steer souls toward safety.

Choir angels range from 4000-4999. Any musical highlight needed is supplied by this choir of heavenly vocalists.

Lessons in the archangel division (000-999) are experience-based, so that the elicited responses enhance and deepen the understanding between angels and humans.

Individual angels launch into adventures on or near the planet Earth, thus achieving understanding through tactile experience.

This novice experience training (NET) is reserved for the archangel grouping.

The learning itself is an important concept for angels to understand.

Humans learn through example and experience, so mimicking that need is the lesson.

Learning is a process.

No one, human or angelic, comes into sentience with a full grasp of knowledge. Coaching is necessary.

The training in NET Adventures (novice experience training) requires angels to take human form in a protective "suit."

All NET suits are numbered.

That ensures that unauthorized sightings can be recorded and later erased from limited human memory by dream redirection during the mandatory human sleep cycle restoring daily balance to the individual.

What would constitute a well-rounded education for an angelic being of level one at Angel Academy?

Knowing why one is learning sets a true compass beginning.

The lessons add to the skill level and align with the possibilities of successful application. Learning creates pathways and strengthens connections.

Angels, like humans, enjoy learning, especially when it is experiential, assumption-challenging, and connected to foundational need.

Angel Academy accepts the challenge of expanding the horizons of students whose needs are negligible but whose desire is to assist others in becoming their most actualized selves.

Angels

- invite the balance; humans choose to respond or ignore.
- meet humans where they exist and open possibilities to connect with the universal balance.
- channel the natural yearnings of humans to become balanced.

Angels collect the seven keys (sight, hearing, tasting, smelling, touching, sensing, and contacting) needed for graduation as archangels from Angel Academy.

Each key category has a series of NET adventures.
Fulfillment must be demonstrated with results.

CHAPTER TWO

Suddenly an angel appeared, and a light shone in the cell.
Acts 12:7a

Sight and the Angels

The human body is incredibly busy when working at full capacity.

Did you know that humans blink an average of fifteen times a minute? Angels do not need to blink. They must practice the skill to grasp the simple task.

Human forms, whether sleeping or awake, perform endless maintenance from waste disposal to eye moisture.

The body has over fifty sphincter muscles to handle the tasks! The balance needed to keep things positive is staggering.

Eyes alone are a marvel of innovation.

Light enters through the black spot in the center, the pupil, which can alter its size to match the light entering.

The iris, the colored part around it, shrinks or grows with the muscle movement.

Light then passes to the retina at the back of the eye which turns light into signals that the brain can understand.

The two eyes give the brain slightly different angles ensuring depth perception.

The brain then figures out what the eye is seeing.

Special mention should be afforded to eyebrows and eyelashes protecting the eye–one from brow sweat and one from particles in the environment.

Eyelids also keep the surface clean and moist, along with the glands that eliminate germs and dust through tears.

Many of the body's sensory receptors are in the eyes.

The eyeball itself is irregularly spherical (like the zero) and hollow with fluids to hold its shape.

Sight can be defined both as a feat of the amazing eye taking in images and as the inspiration that arises from mentally scrutinizing what is viewed.

One sees with the eyes and with the mind.
Angels need both lessons to be most helpful to humans.

Eyesight is strictly an experience-based activity.

Angels can listen to humans discuss what they see or can ask for specific NET missions to add to the sight knowledge.

The mechanics of sight are easily noted.

The interpretation of what is seen is a completely different phenomenon.

Light itself is electromagnetic radiation traveling in waves.

Insight, however, is the act of seeing into a situation in a penetrating way. Thoughts can be intuitive or simply practical.

As far as your eyes are concerned, what you "see" does not read good or bad. It just exists because light allows an image to be sent to the brain.

It is the brain that interprets the meaning of the image. Experience prompts the mind to think that something is either a plus or a minus, a positive or a negative, an addition to be treasured or an intrusion to be shunned.

The eye makes no judgement, it simply delivers.

No matter what is seen, it needs to be interpreted.

A child may stand at a holiday decoration and be drawn to sing a favored tune stirred to the forefront by the scene.

Others standing by can look and see it as sinister or embarrassing to feel forced to join in the singing at the time.

Some may ridicule, others may be comforted.

Insight allows sight to be directed in an informed manner.

It requires grappling with the variations available to the observer.

A crying infant can signal annoyance to one, empathy to another, action to a third, physical violence to a fourth.

Eyes do not decide, brains do.

Sight, insight, and inspiration are all wrapped in the desire for balance in the brain.

The idea is to attempt to be present to the choices.

Angels can be called to help balance the responses of daily life.

Insight can be applied so that large choices in a positive direction can lead to smaller choices that support the overall flow.

Sight can be the opening sense to establish direction.

One ingenious innovation in the human form is the need to sleep.

Humans unconsciously reflect on the decisions of the day and then, when waking, consciously choose to remain the same or change.

Angels are available to assist even when humans sleep. They do not need refreshment and therefore remain on call as it were.

Sight, insight, and inspiration are means to self-understanding.

If a human needs assistance, calling on an angel is always an option.

Seeing clearly is the first of seven keys needed to graduate from the program at Angel Academy.

Razi 212

I like to wear a mask when I land to invite all of my senses to see.

It may seem strange at first but I have found that relying on my eyes alone limits perception.

The ground is a little warm and so the sun must have been visible. I smell the faintest hint of lavender, and sense moisture in the air, a little rotting scent and oh a rock where I placed a hand.

It must be late in the day, the birds are pretty quiet and a few insects are in the background. Now I notice a root under my suit and if I scoot along perhaps a tree will make itself known.

Since the air has some moisture this is not a desert or a mountain or winter or near a shore. A moment more and I will guess.

I do enjoy this exercise. Guessing always delivers the thrill of insightful knowledge.

Now let me concentrate – rooted plants, dry soil, moisture in air, birds, bees, insects, warmth from a day's sun, scent of rot, lavender, rosemary and a little plum. I can hear birds, insects and small creatures moving about.

Maybe I should taste something, then again maybe not. That did not work out well the last outing.

Well my guess would be near a fruit tree in a grove at the early evening on the southern part of the northern continent. Time to look!

Wow, it really is beautiful here. What a great play of color — so many wildflowers.

Justice to a place requires using all methods of gathering before viewing the whole picture. I will remember that lesson.

The Archangel Raziel is the "justice of God." Raziel can help to find the root of a just solution to difficulties. Ask for assistance from Raziel to solve mysteries and "see" solutions.

CHAPTER THREE

The angel said to me in the dream,
'Jacob.' I answered, 'Here I am.'
Genesis 31:11

Hearing and the Angels

The human ear is an elegant system.

Sound makes waves, tunnels the vibrations to the eardrum, moves through the smallest bones in the human body into the inner ear where the physical vibrations are converted into electrical impulses so the brain can identify them as sound.

If that 'sounds' complicated, it is.

Air is converted to sound which is further identified by pitch, volume, and familiarity.

The complexity of the ear is a study in threes, three main parts move sound through three sets of three – bones, cochlea sections and canals for equilibrium.

There are three bones in the middle ear, three chambers in the cochlea inner ear and three semicircular canals to control and identify equilibrium.

Waves of sound travel through air on the outside of the body and into the ear drum and then are amplified to move through the liquid of the inner ear.

Infrasound is too low for human ears and ultrasound too high.

There are people who hear nothing because the ear mechanisms don't function as they were designed.

A famous example of a non-hearing person hearing anyway is Ludwig van Beethoven (1770-1827).

History established that Beethoven was deaf from birth and yet his contribution to music is unequaled.

Stories are told of how he took the legs off the piano and lay on the floor to feel the vibrations to compose.

Amazing if fact, but true enough that hearing is a wider skill that can be achieved in unconventional ways.

Angels are known to sing and listen; one must assume there is a means involved although it does not necessitate the limitations of human hearing.

Imagination may be a component.

Humans can use their minds to hear things from the past or to relive a key event.

Some people even report 'ear worms' that repeat endlessly and may drive to distraction.

Angels do not have the same limited hearing as humans so they need to undergo activities driven by the human experience of listening.

Amazing insights could aid in communication between the two groups.

The sounds of words or music are just one aspect of the overall sensation of hearing. One must interpret what is heard, read facial and environmental cues to ascertain what is real or unreal, beneath the words or between.

If the question is asked- How are you feeling today? – the cues change the meaning. It could be assessing pain management, be a romantic overture, an assessment of depression or happiness, an invitation to share information or an invitation to torture. The facial and surrounding context changes the meaning drastically.

Non-human beings must encounter hearing and its interpretation to really understand. That is where the NET adventures fill the gaps by allowing context to be experienced firsthand.

Angels have much to learn in dealing effectively with humans, just as the ear has much to do with maintaining a sense of body equilibrium.

Three small semicircular canals above the cochlea are the center of balance.

Deep in the skull, protected by bone, they curve to solve sensory conflict so that up and down can be identified keeping the entire body system in functioning order.

Think that is a small feat?

Ask someone with balance issues and be assured that without this small contribution to the whole package, every task is compromised.

Archangels are eager to hear like humans so that interpreting what will be most helpful is possible.

The lesson of human hearing is the second of the seven keys to master understanding.

Ari 419

SPLASHDOWN!!!

"That was awesome!" Ari exclaimed as the saltwater hugged the suit and kissed the face.

"Seawater is amazing!"

"It is another world down here."

Ari paused to listen as the splash diminished.

"Quiet," Ari thought as turning became the next action, "quiet."

But then a low, long chord drew attention behind where Ari poised.

The hum continued, slowly washing over the antennae but no creature was in sight.

The pitch changed, the sound moved, up and down, high and low.

Ari was tempted to follow the song but decided against it when a little creature, attached to a nearby seagrass bed, caught the attention.

"You are a seahorse," Ari declared. "You are magnificent!"

The creature kept one eye peeled on Ari as the other continued scanning. Seahorses have excellent vision. Their eyes are independent and able to rotate completely around.

"Can you talk to me? I just want to learn about you."

The seahorse remained silent for a bit and then declared, "Don't block the way. I eat things that float by me and you are distracting me!"

"Surely, you can wait a few minutes."

"That's how much you know. I must eat constantly to stay alive. When you have no teeth and no stomach, you cannot wait to eat!"

"Sorry, I meant no harm. I was curious because you are so interesting."

"Swim on and go look for someone with time on their hands. Between eating constantly and raising fry (seahorse babies), I am too busy for idle chat."

Ari surveyed the scene. Seagrasses with young animals hiding were abundant as well as blue-green and red algae.

Just then Ari noticed something moving about below, slinking, actually.

"Wow! What is that?"

It looked like a bubble with two eyes gliding over the coral. There were arms to and fro helping the creature move effortlessly.

"I believe that is an octopus," Ari remarked. "It looks so smooth and glassy."

Suddenly, the color changed to match the darker hue of a mound.

"Camouflage, that is the sparkliest thing I have seen so far."

"Hello, hello."

The octopus stopped, matched the texture of the rock being crossed, and disappeared.

"I have never seen anything so crazy. I would not even know that was a creature if I hadn't seen it with my own eyes."

"Who are you?" the annoyed octopus inquired.

"I am Ari 419, a visitor here for novice explorer training (NET). I was flying overhead and noticed this magnificent underwater world, so I stopped to take a closer look."

"Do you enjoy the taste of seafood?"

"I have never had any and do not require food. You are safe with me."

"Just checking. Would you like to know what you are admiring?"

"Absolutely," Ari replied.

"Well, this is a coral reef. I once heard it referred to as 'the rainforest of the sea'. Coral reefs cover only 1% of the briny deep but support 25% of all ocean life."

"How did you learn that?"

"Well, one of my pals is a turtle who lays eggs on the beach. He is a good listener and apparently the two-legged creatures do a lot of talking."

"I am an octopus. You have seen my dynamic camouflage, but I also protect myself with black ink and can swim extremely fast. I have excellent sight, which is how I spotted you."

"Thanks so much for all the information. You are exquisite! I especially like the way you slither over everything. Who else would you recommend I see on this flight?"

"Perhaps you should stick to creatures with brains so conversation is at least possible. Dolphins, crabs, starfish, clownfish or my friend the green turtle would be interesting."

"How about that sound I heard earlier? Who was that?"

"Oh, that was a humpback whale. They love to sing and the sound carries for miles so they may not be close enough to see. You can't miss them though because they are huge but totally harmless, unless you are krill or small fish!"

"You have been such a fun creature to meet. While floating here I have been watching the jellies jet around, the clownfish dart, the dolphins overhead. This coral reef is quite a find."

"Oh, it is and that is why you must stop and watch to really see everything. While waiting, the hundreds of creatures relax and go about their routines. It is the only way to find out what is really happening."

"My friend the green turtle is on route here and will tell you about land and sea existence. Our biggest threat is the two-legged land creatures living near the ocean."

"Happy travels Ari 419."

Ari continued watching the scene.

"This place is a spectacular example of cooperation, balance and strength! Totally different species live in harmony, relying on one another. They each demonstrate their usefulness and the whole thrives."

While thinking, Ari's wristlet trembled, and on it appeared a seahorse, an octopus, and a musical note - reminders of this underwater adventure.

The green sea turtle told Ari to hang onto its shell until the shore appeared. What a fabulous experience with the wristlet charms to capture the magic!

The coral reef is a magnificent ecosystem, and quietly paying attention made all the difference.

ARI 419, upon graduation from Angel Academy, will become ARIEL, the archangel who loves the environment and its creatures. She is a fierce defender of Earth. Ariel instills in humans a desire to care for the environment, motivating them to work together to improve the Earth's cooperation.

CHAPTER FOUR

Then he lay down under the bush and fell asleep.
All at once an angel touched him and said,
"Get up and eat." 1 Kings 19:5

Tasting and the Angels

Humans may take for granted the sensation of eating and drinking because it is an activity repeated with such regularity.

Sometimes a meal is memorable, but most are not.

They are necessary for body maintenance and cannot be put aside if the expectation is long life and prosperous times.

The possibilities to complete the task of nourishing the body are given to all.

Humans decide daily how to attend to the duty.

Eating/tasting begins with the mouth and the tongue.

The tongue is a muscle in the mouth that detects temperature, texture, and flavors.

It senses if something is chewy or oily.

It even identifies rancid, bitter items so that they will be discarded before swallowing and harming the body.

The tongue is covered in bumps or papillae.

Taste buds are in the walls of the bumps.

Each bud is filled with teeny tasting hairs to sense the flavor and send signals to the brain to identify the taste.

Smell is an important factor as well. The two are connected to effectively work the tasting system.

Five flavors can be detected equally well around the tongue, but the sides may be more sensitive than the midsection.

The five main flavors are sweet, salty, bitter, sour, and umami,

a savory detector.

It has been estimated that taste is 80% smell so the olfactory receptors must be mentioned.

Taste and smell together can trigger emotions and activate memories to alert to danger or revive past experiences.

Have you ever walked into a home and remarked that it smells like Christmas?

The senses draw the mind back to a previous and hopefully positive experience.

Smell and taste together team up to both remind, restore, and extend.

The mouth actually waters when the smell is identified.

The human tongue also aids in turning solid food into a mash, with the support of the teeth of course.

Talking is another natural activity aided by the tongue and teeth.

The front of the tongue muscle is flexible and used to create many sounds.

A dry mouth can't make effective sound and a dry tongue can't taste anything.

Ask anyone who has tried public speaking with a dry mouth. It is difficult to mask well but can be remedied with moisture almost immediately.

Tasting is complex and, like the other senses, involves sending information for the brain to interpret and categorize.

In fact, each taste bud can detect five flavors and can send messages to different sections of the brain for identification.

Think about that.

The brain is varied enough to receive such information and interpret it with accuracy and speed.

Humans must seek nourishment and moisture to maintain a balanced tasting system.

Angels do not experience that need.

It is important, however, that angels encounter tasting so that the relationship can be further cemented between the two.

Humans spend a lot of time in body maintenance regarding food and drink.

Some overindulge and some lack access.

Angels must have at least a rudimentary understanding of the requirements and their impact on humans.

How can one aid a species without knowing a fundamental need imbedded into their very core?

NET adventures then must include the sensation of talking, tasting, and smelling.

Each angel needs to be open to the variety of possibilities when using the tongue for speech and eating.

Practice must occur.

Finding humans who are willing to share their experiences may be difficult if angelic forms revealed the quest.

It is most effective when children share their thoughts, not only because their tongues are twice as sensitive to taste as adults but also because their fear of friends, visible and invisible, is minimal and usually accepted by adults as fantasy.

Angels can gather intel from youth and extrapolate the meaning to enhance encounters with more experienced humans.

Non-human Earth species have tongues as well.

Blue whales have the largest weighing 2.7 metric tons, the weight of an elephant!

Giraffes have tongues that are bluish-purple and coated in thick antiseptic saliva. Their tongues can wrap around things and grasp them, pulling them into the mouth.

Woodpeckers have tongues that wrap around their skull and chameleon tongues are twice as long as their bodies.

Tongues have allowed sea creatures to become land animals and are an amazing muscle whether chewing, speaking, or silently expressing oneself by sticking it out.

Angels need to encounter the experience of the tongue so that human behavior gains clarity.

It is the third of seven keys needed to graduate from Angel Academy in the Archangel division.

CHAPTER FIVE

There the angel appeared to him in
flames of fire from within a bush.
Exodus 3:2

Smelling and the Angels

Now the angels move to mastering the sense that surrounds all the pungent human memories- the nose.

No one forgets the smells of life!

They bring to light one of the absolute delights of being human.

The nose is a simple mechanism, but without it working properly, so much is lost.

First, let's discuss it as the opening that allows the lungs to give the body renewed oxygen and expel what is no longer necessary —a skill taken for granted but quite literally life-sustaining.

Breathing is usually not thought about until it is blocked by the body placed in water, in a small space, or confounded with a head cold.

Breathing must occur many times a minute to keep bodies manageable and alive.

The nose then is the gateway to the entire respiratory system.

Air enters the dual nostrils, moves through the nasal cavity, down to the windpipe, and ends in the dual lungs.

The nose moistens air, warms, and filters it before the air travels deeper into the body.

The mucus membrane in the nasal cavity even traps dust, germs, and foreign substances to keep things out of the lungs.

For a rhythm that keeps the body in working order, it is at once a simple and complicated passage.

Sneezing, which removes problem substances, happens at one hundred miles per hour! That is a remarkable feat for a body that doesn't even have to move in space to accomplish the sneeze.

Second, consider the sense of smell.

It is the first sense available when a human is born, working before seeing and hearing even engage.

Smells can trigger a fight or flight response, make the mouth water with anticipation, recall the memory of someone, or something needed like mother's milk.

Smells can awaken emotions in humans.

Imagine what smells do for dogs who have the olfactory epidermis twenty times larger than humans.

Male moths can smell a female ten kilometers away and then there are African elephants who have the best smeller on the entire planet. There was a noted study on elephants avoiding land mines in Angola suggesting that the scent of the materials in mines was associated with danger causing the species to avoid the smell and remain unharmed.

Specially trained dogs can sniff and screen for diabetes, cancer, and epilepsy in human subjects. The nose knows!

Humans have a yellow pituitary gland that captures smell and then the information travels to the brain through the olfactory nerve until the brain identifies it.

Humans can detect up to 10,000 different scents.

Children have a stronger connection to smell than adults and can distinguish them even further.

The brain, when using sight and hearing, sends signals to a relay center and then out to the proper stations.

Smelling, however, takes a direct route to the brain which has forty million receptor neurons for smells that are replaced every four to six weeks.

No other sense has such a turnover!

Smell is fundamental to human life.

Certainly, it is an experience that angels need so that their understanding is enhanced.

Angels do not have senses, so the learning can prove both informative and entertaining.

Imagine suddenly smelling after the sense has been vacated. The world would seem different with human smells attached to every activity.

Smells can be broken into ten scent categories:

- **Fragrant** (florals and perfumes)
- **Fruity** (all non-citrus fruits)
- **Citrus** (lemon, lime, orange)
- **Woody and resinous** (pine or freshly cut grass)
- **Chemical** (ammonia, bleach)
- **Sweet** (chocolate, vanilla, caramel)
- **Minty and peppermint** (eucalyptus and camphor)
- **Toasted and nutty** (popcorn, peanut butter, almonds)
- **Pungent** (blue cheese, cigar smoke)
- **Decay** (rotting meat, sour milk)

Other aromas, like baked goods or brewing coffee, arc amalgams of two or more of these ten elements. (Jason Castro, Arvind Ramanathan, and Chakra Chennubhotla)

It is worth noting that smells may be offensive to some humans but not to others.

Limburger cheese is pungent but to native eaters it reminds them of fabulous, family, Sunday brunch.

Angels need exposure to the rich and complex world of odors because it is so much a part of the human experience.

Smelling is the fourth key needed for graduation from the Archangel division of Angel Academy.

CHAPTER SIX

There was a violent earthquake, for an angel came down from heaven and, going to the tomb, rolled back the stone, and sat on it. Matthew 28:2

Touching and the Angels

The sense of touch allows humans to detect the properties of objects in the surrounding world.

Temperature, shape, softness, and pain can be perceived by the largest organ in the body – the skin.

Nerve endings send information to the brain for interpretation.

The only skin maintenance required for keeping this system in order is regular washing for cleansing, avoidance of the direct rays of the sun, and the disinfection of any breaches like cuts.

Skin is equipped to maintain itself and grow for many years.

Since skin covers the entire body surface, the sense of touch is not restricted to one part as with eyes, nose, ears, or mouth, but the fingertips, lips, and face have more nerve endings than the rest.

Skin accounts for 16% of the body's weight and no diet can reduce that percentage!

Skin has three main layers, the epidermis or outside, the dermis and the hypodermis. The three work together and function separately as well.

The epidermis is the outermost layer protecting the body from bacteria and virus.

Pores let the oxygen out and the sweat pass.

This barrier is waterproof and every four weeks the cells are replaced by new cells moving up and forcing the older cells to drop off the body.

This layer is also responsible for setting the skin tone by regulating the level of melanin. The more melanin, the darker the skin, and the less susceptible to sun irritation.

Darker skin tones developed in people living in equatorial earth sections for protection from sun harm.

The dermis has hair follicles, sweat glands and nerve endings.

It is the middle skin layer with receptors to collect information from the world outside the body to be sent to the brain for action.

Some receptors detect pressure, some object size and shape, some cold or warmth.

Millions of tiny nerve endings relay information about textures and temperatures and carry the sensations to the brain for analysis.

Skin is the first line of protection against the outside environment, so the electrical impulses sent via the spinal cord relay important messages about heat, cold, pain, and pressure.

The innermost component is the hypodermis; the subcutaneous layer made of fat and connective tissue.

All hair growth happens here, and hair grows everywhere on the human body except palms of the hands and soles of the feet.

Hypodermis also regulates body temperature and is the layer that separates the skin organ from other internal organs functioning in the body.

Skin seals off the insides and absorbs pressure and shock with flexible collagen.

At any time, five percent of the body's blood is circulating through the skin in the dermis layer.

Why spend so much time talking about the skin?

It is the organ perceived by the world and by the human inside.

It shapes thoughts about the inhabitant and by the person as well.

Skin and appearance help others to decide if the person housed is worthwhile for interaction and it turns out the outward appearance is not really in the control of the human at all.

The maintenance is certainly a concern, but the random nature of the appearance is subject to a series of factors assigned by environmental conditions, familial blood lines, and chance encounters.

Touch is a human quality.

Touching another physically is an informative experience and touching emotionally a separate topic.

Humans can use touch to assess the environment, to work with or against the space outside the body, to interact with others to create and build both small and large projects.

Touching surfaces to prepare food is one activity, bathing an infant or aged parent another, playing games a third.

Interaction requires touching and one learns what is necessary and appropriate by following the norms and examples of others.

Touch is a necessary component of human life.

Angels can easily observe this and encounter it in their travels.

Touching emotionally is another matter altogether.

Emotional interactions require a myriad of experiences to interpret.

Humans of all ages seem to continue to learn this art throughout their lifetime.

Words and motions must be combined to initiate, maintain, and continue growing relationships among humans.

People need to agree over and over to continue the path of touching emotionally and some never really get the art of the touch quite right.

One clear thing is that humans are complicated in this area.

Children rely on touch for care and when growing the need changes until they seek it again in exclusivity and then that changes.

The ebb and flow are tough to teach to angelic beings.

Some thoroughly enjoy learning to touch others and food and drink while some are shy about it.

Humans are much the same.

Some touch others constantly and some as little as possible.

The key to learning touch can be found in the cross-section of human interaction.

Angels must be cognizant of the environment and use cues to regulate their touch interactions and emotional touching as seems appropriate.

Humans navigate the same waters but assess almost daily what situations call forth around physical and emotional touching.

The skin organ, though complex in nature, is the simplest part of learning the art of touching.

Angels will have to spend a great deal of their NET adventure time earning the key for the sense of touch.

CHAPTER SEVEN

The angel said to him, "I am Gabriel. I stand in the presence of God, and I have been sent to speak to you and to tell you this good news." Luke 1:19

Sensing and the Angels

Humans live in a world of senses, governed by what can be seen, heard, smelled, touched, eaten, engaged.

It is what is known as sensate knowledge, and the entire species seems consumed by it.

Stress is the unifier of the senses allowing the brain to decide daily whether to run, fight, or hide.

Humans watch clocks and deadlines and live between commercials and needs.

Stress is the controller, and negative thoughts, the guides.

It is true that humans are constructed to have senses and to pay attention as they change and interact with the environment.

Senses determine reality with the brain constantly scanning to maintain control.

Anxiety exists to promote survival.

It makes sense in the moment.

One must then remember what happens when needs are met, and the present environment is not one of disarray.

Some people fill the void by watching others who are not so lucky. Scary movies, videos, reality tv, sporting events are distractions to stay in the state of insecurity even if it is controlled.

Stress narrows the focus so freedom from stress must open to possibilities to determine new reality and to connect with a wholeness that cannot be achieved in the bump and grind of daily life.

Humans can take attention from schedules, time, and self-promotion to connect to new energy and to become familiar with a new reality.

This could prove to be a contagious energy that orders the other world in new and exciting ways.

The beginning of existence was a balance beyond a single self.

It was a present moment, a transitional moment, a unity of clear intention.

It is the energy at the heart of matter that creates coherence and leads to harmony.

Angels live in that existence and invite humans to become familiar with the availability beyond the senses.

Angels use repetition to gain human attention and invite new realities through signs and their presence.

Meditation is a door for some.

Art, music, dance, and writing for others brings the same feeling.

Angels invite constantly.

Angels are always ready to lead.

It is the sixth key earned to complete the sensate path to knowledge.

Follow the guideline below if you wish to experience meditation and meet the balance.

Ask the angels for guidance.

You can meet some of them in the next chapter.

INDIVIDUAL REFLECTION

1. Find a spot where you will not be disturbed. Outside is good for some if the noise around is minimal and your presence will not be intrusive/inviting to others. Inside is good for some if a place of peace can be found where no one will disturb, and all equipment and devices can be completely turned off. That includes devices receiving spoken commands and phones, dryers etc. All screens are black for the time. (Hang a do not disturb sock on the door.)
2. Set a timer for 20 minutes to 30 minutes so no temptation to check clocks will exist. This eliminates wondering and promotes attention to the exercise at hand.
3. Have a working pen with a notebook.
4. Date the entry with month/day/year.
5. Begin by sitting comfortably.
6. Close your eyes.
7. Repeat one mantra – a seven syllable thought that can be spoken half on the breath in and half on the breath out. Slowly over and over.

Sample mantras follow. (calm is a gift to receive) (peace is a wave over me) (awareness increases life) (quiet and calm invite life)

8. Breathe slowly and relax. Repeat a mantra.
9. When a sense of calm is achieved, read the reflection on the next page slowly several times. SLOWLY
10. Think about its meaning.
11. Write/draw any thoughts in the notebook, even if they seem random.
12. Allow time to reflect.
13. Write a mantra – a 7-word phrase – that is about the reading or the reflection.
14. Repeat thi mantra until the time is completed. Carry the mantra with you by repeating silently no matter where you are until the next reflection time.

A tree that it takes both arms to encircle grew from a tiny rootlet. A many storied pagoda is built by placing one brick upon another brick. A journey of three thousand miles is begun by a single step.   Lao-Tzu

Mantra: Help me step into the light.

CHAPTER EIGHT

Angels speak to those who silence
their minds long enough to hear.

Contacting the Angels

When students graduate with the seven keys, the last one is the presentation of what each can bring to humans as a gift. The explanations below may help connect to the angels who have the Seven Keys!

(Remember – EL is added to the end of each graduate's name and means "of God")

Archangel Michael   (Micha 106)   Defender of God

aura – royal blue   crystal – sugalite (pink to purple mineral)

Michael is a stalwart archangel who guards the righteous against any dark forces. If you need protection from harm, Michael is a powerful ally. Call on Michael to enter your waking or dreaming to impart strength and courage, to stand up fiercely for what is right.

Archangel Haniel   (Hani 189)   Joy of God

aura – bluish white   crystal – protective gem moonstone

Haniel is associated with the moon and with nurturing energy. When the moon shines brightly on a crisp evening one can feel the rays caressing the scene with sustaining energy and that is the joy of Haniel. Call on this angel to gain clarity when things are cloudy and ask for the joy associated with purpose and surety. Let the moon beams shine into the windows at night as an invitation to Haniel.

Archangel Raziel   (Razi 212)   Justice of God

aura – colors of the rainbow   crystal – clear quartz (crystal clarity)

Raziel is the angel who enjoys balance at the heart of every situation. Justice is the balance of all sides and if you seek the sweet spot of the center, call on Raziel to help you to find it and live in it. Raziel likes the rainbow because it represents the perfect bridge. Call Raziel to see the center clearly and to manifest the balance in relationships and duties.

Archangel Raphael   (Rapha 259)   Healer of God

aura – emerald green   crystal – green fluorite healing crystal

Raphael is seen as the angelic physician, the one who heals people and relationships. Raphael can even inspire humans to care for themselves by nudging toward preventative measures and moderation. Every being needs healing at some time. Raphael is available for emotional, physical, and psychological balance. Ask for the assistance and then in subtle ways the healing can begin. Invitations toward the balance must be accepted to begin the work.

Archangel Jophiel   (Jophi 333)   Beauty of God

aura – light yellow   crystal – citrine crystal stone

Sometimes it is easy to be caught in the rush of life and this angel, Jophiel, reminds that one needs to slow down and enjoy the natural beauty around whether it is snow, rain, sunshine, or wind. Each setting and season hold the beauty of the balance. One must stop considering it, if only for a few moments. The balance of the environment reminds us of all the beauty available in relationships with the self and others. Ask Jophiel to open your mind to the possibilities of seeing beauty.

Archangel Gabriel   (Gabri 339)   Strength of God

aura – pinkish orange (copper)   crystal – quartz deep citrine

Think of all the life situations that require strength of character and then the range of Gabriel can be appreciated. Personal power is given to develop the inner child and to parent adopted and biological children. Gabriel loves announcing events, so writers and journalists are also favored guests for attention. Strength is the core of balance and Gabriel is the strength. Ask for whatever is needed to conduct yourself with clarity and love, Gabriel will lead the parade toward the best self.

Archangel Ariel   (Ari 419)   Lion of God

Aura – rose pink   crystal – rose quartz

Bravery and courage are the heart of the angel Ariel. If you need to focus on summoning a backbone to perform necessary tasks, then asking Ariel will assure that you are traveling forward with the heart of a lion. Ariel is synonymous with strength and this angel will stay with you through whatever event you need assistance. Ariel is faithful to the calling and never abandons the post. Ask Ariel for whatever is needed to promote good.

Archangel Uriel   (Uri 421)   Light of God

aura – pale yellow   crystal – amber stone

What is light if not the absence of all darkness? Uriel brings clarity of insight, answers, information, and guidance for the intellect. Every human seeks to know what the best road will be or the best path to follow. Uriel is the one to shed some insight on all inquiries. Ask Uriel to guide the dreams while sleeping so that information becomes clear in the light of day. Uriel can open doors to see what is real and true.

Archangel Azrael   (Azra 555)   Helper of God

aura – creamy vanilla   crystal – yellow calcite

Sometimes Azrael is called an angel of death because helping humans review their lives is part of the character of this beautiful angel. Everyone needs to have a life check up to see where one has been and where one is going. Azrael can facilitate whether the person is seeking to make decisions for the future or if they need assistance crossing from the physical plane of existence to the next. Azrael comforts the dying and those in attendance of them and when asked will offer comfort in dreams of passed loved ones. Azrael is on call for counselors to aid their journeys with the living and the dying.

Archangel Raguel   (Ragu 619)   Friend of God

Aura – pale blue   crystal – aquamarine

Raguel does exactly what a good friend should, ensures harmony, cooperation, and order among all with deep feeling. Raguel encourages all to act in ways that are fair and just so that each one feels cared for and loved. Call on this angel to guide friendships and to repair relationships but do not be surprised if the repair must start with one's own attitudes!

Archangel Zadkiel   (Zadki 624)   Righteousness of God

Aura – deep blue   crystal – lapis lazuli

Anyone carrying heavy emotional burdens needs to speak immediately to Zadkiel. This angel wants to lead humans to the center of the answers, to the balance of emotions, to stability. Emotional healing and forgiving are the core of Zadkiel. This angel will work to clear layers of distress whether you are dreaming or awake. Ask for the assistance of Zadkiel to make right what is less than right.

Archangel Jeremiel   (Jeremi 629)   Mercy of God

Aura – deep purple   crystal – amethyst

Respect is at the heart of the angel Jeremiel. Every human deserves positive handling by others but not all receive it. Jeremiel will help individuals to show mercy to others and to act in ways that promote the trait in families and work environments. When mercy is the compass, responses to situations are changed. Jeremiel will help mercy to be part of all experiences through early life to death. Ask for help to live a life of mercy and to feel the mercy of the angels.

Archangel Chamuel   (Chamu 726)   Seeker of God

Aura – pale green   crystal – green fluorite

Everyone needs a friend who can help to find things or people who are lost. Chamuel is such a companion. Whether finding a career path that will assure happiness or a person to match wits, Chamuel is the master of finding it all. Call on Chamuel day or night to bring a companion for the journey through life. Dreams may help to shape a true direction on the path to positive living. Green is the color of life and Chamuel wants to lead to everything growing and alive.

The final key to graduation from Angel Academy for archangels is the ability to translate the balance at the core of existence to the lives of humans. Once an archangel can define their contribution, they have the final key!

Angelic beings remain ever available to human calls for assistance. Each archangel has a domain of specialty for which they open the communication.

Angels desire to help humans to balance their life responses so that all are invited to experience a positive existence internally which hopefully will lead to one externally.

CHAPTER NINE

NET ADVENTURES

Ragu 619

"Oh, the earth feels so warm today!"

Ragu dropped to the ground and the view of the sky became a panorama.

"The grass is soft and smells wonderfully sweet. I wish I could lie here forever!"

Suddenly an ant appeared on the belly of Ragu's suit, walking as if the world were there for the sheer pleasure of the stroll.

"Well," thought Ragu, "if there is one ant, there will be others around in no time."

Instead of moving, Ragu decided to see what would happen. After all, the suit protected the body so what was there to lose except the sheer wonderment of the next moments.

Seconds passed and soon an ant family was marching in a row.

It was as if Ragu was blocking the one road available. The ants had to stay on course to complete the mission no matter the changing landscape.

As Ragu watched the march, none of the ants even noticed the rounded presence inside the suit being crossed.

"That is kind of funny," Ragu thought, "not even seeing that the obstacle is movable."

Suddenly, Ragu decided to shake a bit and every ant ignored the change. Marching continued unabated.

Time passed and the steady stream of ants continued.

Ragu began to ask if it was right to block the way of creatures for one's own pleasure because they seem small and inconsequential. Should not the larger yield to the smaller for the sake of the good of all concerned? Then Ragu's understanding of such a small matter exploded to the universe and its extensions.

Isn't it right for the large to watch out for the small?

Isn't it important for choices to be made that protect not harm even the least among us?

What could be more vital than justice lived rightly?

I must remember the lesson of the ants.

Moving gently through the space occupied, it may be home to the unseen who in time could reshape everything for the good of all.

Quiet reflection allows one to see even the small creatures that are part of the whole.

Ants are creatures with a group mentality and I need to remember to think communally too!

The Archangel Raguel is the "justice of God." Raguel works to enhance communication between people and seeks the best solutions in every situation. Raguel even watches the other angels so as to enhance their skills for promoting positive change and good order. Ask Raguel for help with issues of justice and harmony.

Rapha 259

"Wind, I always loved wind," Rapha remarked.

"Movement and the unexpected gusts that blow up milkweed and shake grasses.

Maybe it is the noise of it all.

Too much can destroy but, on a lovely day, wind wakes the trees and makes even the lowly smile sweetly and admire what they cannot see."

"Not everything real can be observed, some things, the best things, can only be sensed or felt in a fleeting way.

Love is beyond words, fun is hard to explain, reality is apparent only to the one noticing it, just like the wind.

Elusive, fun-loving, inviting, unpredictable but affecting everything in its path. Sounds like the definition of a good friend!"

"One day when I was young, I was sitting on a cloud just admiring the view.

The fluffy mass below me was happily floating on a breeze and I was watching other clouds around me changing, growing, becoming all kinds of shapes.

What a perfect little day I was enjoying and then, suddenly, a dark storm started charging into view. Not just a happy little shower but a mania of thunder, lightning, hail, and water. Faster and faster, it approached and with alarm I sat up to consider what to do. I cannot change the storm. My powers do not lie in that realm. I could find another angel who could effect the change but urgency prevented such an action.

Below I could see alarm building in the faces of the people on earth. They were beginning to scatter and run as the fuss of the storm approached with lightning and thunder announcing their arrival. Louder and louder, shaking all in its wake, the noise continued.

The happy little cloud I was seated on moved to let the action travel past and said to me, "Don't worry Rapha, some clouds just love to carry on and watch everyone run for cover. They are so powerful! Look at how they push, stretch, and destroy! But remember, smiles will rule the day and lovely clouds will continue to dominate by hugging the earth gently and floating on the wings of wind."

Sure enough, after a time, the storm blew its last breath.

"See that" said the cloud, "it is all over."

"Everything will settle down and you can relax, Rapha."

"Just remember not to take the blowhards too seriously, they run out of steam eventually but, most importantly, learn to appreciate the clouds who silently drift on the winds most days."

Raphael is a fun-loving archangel who handles relationships with others and in families. Raphael whose name means "God Heals" can help promote communication, love, and any healing needed in the body and spirit including the detoxification of both. Ask!

HANI 189

Hani paused in the black sky to admire the winking stars.

The moon was full here and the other sky creatures enjoyed the glow.

Hani smiled at the scene.

What is it about the balance of space?

So full of possibilities.

It is the mix of movement and stillness.

Things explode, implode, change, adapt but most find a middle and hold it.

Why?

Hani decided to ask the stars.

Who would know more about it than one born of heated gas and doomed to die in a sky drama? Balance seems the very nature of stars.

Luckily, there was a lovely cluster shining brightly nearby.

"What can you say about finding the center, holding the balance?" Hani asked.

"We spend most of our lives with gravity compression balanced by outward pressure," the star replied.

"We all start as a cloud of gas. Then the gas particles run into one another to create heat energy until the young star produces strong winds and can be seen. Equilibrium allows us to live 90% of our lives shining and then collapse. We certainly seem like the poster child for balance but, Hani, you should ask the moon. That is a balancing act if ever one existed. Not much change there and certainly no way of shining. A rock dangling in the darkness doesn't seem like a pleasant existence but the moon is the epidemy of balance – at least the stars think so."

Hani gazed quietly at the moon. "It is quite beautiful, but it generates no light of its own, no wind, no change for that matter. Why would the stars suggest a discussion with a hunk of rock?"

The moon woke from silence and said,

"When I was young, I had a lot of anxiety."

"How could I accomplish anything worthwhile hanging stationery with nothing to distinguish me from any other space rock? How could I be noticed in this space field of shining objects?"

"I really wasted centuries consumed by self-flagellation."

"I watched planets develop, grow, and die. Stars too. Moving gas balls streaking around, sometimes slamming into me because they were paying no attention. What difference can a rock that looks dead make to the universe?"

"Well, one day, instead of keeping my head down, I looked up and watched and waited in the stillness."

"I began to notice things that I hadn't before."

"I could not generate light, but I felt very beautiful when reflecting it."

"I was a mass of rock, but I had craters and boulders all over that added shimmer to the mirrored glow."

"Water was changed by my pull on the planet closest and even newborns could be coaxed into the moonlight when my fullness was visible.

Moon changes were a rhythm to many creatures watching the patterns.

It seemed I communicated loudly by silently reflecting light."

'My existence was of consequence and, unlike other bodies in space, I could be counted on forever. I mattered."

"I found balance."

"We cannot all be stars or planets or gassy balls of ice. Some are meant to rock the universe shining in their own quiet way, steadily accomplishing what needs to be achieved by the light of the moon."

Hani was pleased with this trip to the heavens and thanked the moon for the wisdom.

"I will remember-

that if you face your fears, you can grow brighter.

that positive communication with yourself leads to greater awareness and that balance is at the center, the rock of happiness."

Hani smiled at the scene and then continued the journey.

The Archangel Haniel is the "joy of God," the divine communicator.

Often associated with the moon, Venus, and the throat chakra for communication, Haniel is the balance of blue and green in turquoise with silver wings. Haniel will increase the ability to speak inner truth effectively if you ask.

Archangel Ariel   (ARI 419)   Lion of God

Ari awakened in the strong arms of an almond tree.

The helmet's antenna was attached somehow to the blossomed branch.

Ari tried freeing the antenna and ahhhhh

suddenly was

falling

to the ground -

humpf.

Pink almond pedals rained down.

"What a place to land," Ari said aloud.

Rows and rows of almond trees stood at measured attention.

"Someone did this on purpose, so someone must not be far from here," Ari announced to the grove of almond trees who listened but did not answer.

"Walking would be wise," Ari thought.

So walking is what happened next.

Walking,

walking,

walking,

more walking and

resting, for a moment,

that turned into waking in the darkness at the edge of the almond grove.

The trees had passed Ari limb to limb.

There was a sound though – a constant sound – not very loud – not very soft – just right for sleeping.

Z Z Z Z ZZZZZZZZZZZZZZZZZZZZZZZZZZZZZZZZ

Good! Sleep Ari------------

The almond trees stood tall and satisfied.

Almond trees are happy most of the time, rooted to the nourishing belly.

You would be to in such a place.

The next day Ari's eyes opened and gazed at a deep, blue bath, just a few feet away from the old tree at the edge of the almond grove.

And on the stump a wristlet- a magical, mystical circle with a bright pink petal attached.

"I want to wear that wristlet."

Ari stood, placed the new band over the left glove, and admired the look of it.

Now what about the blue, blue, liquid triangling everywhere.

Ari, an explorer by nature, went to get a better view.

Blue above,

blue below,

blue from side to side.

It was a sea of blue triangles – flowing, bouncing, upping, and downing, inning and outing, endlessly moving, sounding so musical, tickling Ari's antenna.

"The blue is so wide and so long, I can only see sea."

The wristlet pulled at the gloved hand and Ari was drawn into the blue, blue water.

Walk, Ari, walk!

"Maybe the maker of the almond grove lives on the sea."

It was vast but shallow so Ari walked carefully at first but then without fear.

Sometimes what seems improbable can be made probable – one walking step at a time.

Blue above,

blue below,

everywhere blue and then a ball to hug all the way to the edge.

Ari was passed from wave to wave by the dancing water.

Stepping out of the sea a round blue bead of liquid appeared on the wristlet – that magical, mystical ring now had a very pink almond petal and a deep blue droplet.

Ari was sleepy after such a long journey. The ball formed around Ari's suit, just right for sleeping.

Good! Sleep Ari--------------------

Z Z Z Z ZZZZZZZZZZZZZZZZZZZZZZZZZZZZZZZZZZZZZZ

The triangling waves pointed proudly.

Waves are happy most of the time – clearing, cleansing, carrying whatever is needed.

You would be too in such a place.

Ari woke to find nothing overhead.

As far as the eyes could see everything was colorless.

The slab beneath, the breath of the space surrounding the sky.

Blank

Blank

Blank

Ari sat and then stood turning and turning. There was nothing in any direction.

Panic stirred and then the wristlet moved.

It still had the pink petal from the almond grove and the blue droplet of liquid.

Ari did not dream those visions.

The gloved hand with the wristlet began to lead the way.

Ari stumbled to keep up with the ring until off the ground the boots rose and faster and faster the movement grew.

All at once Ari could fly glove first, swirling up and down, side to side, around and around.

The air was cool

free

strong.

It made a whistling sort of sound over the suit.

The fear started building again.

"What will happen to me?"

The air stopped and so did Ari.

Thump

thump

thump.

It seemed like a long time passed.

Ari was finally calm.

The wristlet moved again and the flying commenced. This time Ari was determined to ignore the fear.

Something appeared in the distance. What could it be? A reddish pool was writhing to the rhythm of the air pulling the wristlet forward until gently setting Ari in the midst. Everything beautiful and touching seemed possible near this reddish pulse. Ari was in the heart of the space. A single tear appeared running along the skin of the heart.

Ari vowed to remember that lesson and as the vow was spoken a red heart appeared on the wristlet next to the pink almond petal and the blue drop of water. The heart had a single tear.

Ari snuggled against the gently beating heart and was lulled to sleep.

Good! Sleep Ari--------------------

Z Z Z Z ZZZZZZZZZZZZZZZZZZZZZZZZZZZZZZZZZZZZZZZZZZ

ZZ

The air swirled gently in and out of Ari's body.

Air is happy most of the time – cleansing, refreshing, soothing.

You would be to if you were free.

Ari was awakened by a crackling sound and discovered the wall in the process of exploring.

The noise was on the other side.

Climbing to the top Ari could see an orange and yellow mass moving over the whole area, peaking, and swirling, rising, and falling.

Ari had no idea until all the dancing color turned dark and someone was working to stop the fire.

"Some conflagration" the voice shouted.

Ari looked all around and saw the almond trees in the distance.

"No worries – the ground recovers and rebuilds"

"In time it will be a rainbow of color again"

"Everything has its time"

Ari's wristlet crackled and on it appeared an orange and yellow flame.

"Earth waits by the water,

water feeds air,

air increases fire,

fire cleanses earth.

Everything is interconnected

all part of the one."

Ari understood and now wanted to continue the journey with the wristlet to remember –

A deep blue droplet

A heart of red

The orange and yellow flame

The pink almond petal and the ring that binds them together.

Carry all the elements to remember.

And don't forget the tear Ari!

Happy, happy travels!

The Archangel Ariel is the one associated with the environment and its protection. Ari, through traveling, became Ariel – the lion of the ONE.

Archangel Ariel   (ARI 419)

"What a session that was!

Cooperation, cooperation, cooperation – is that the only word uttered at Angel Academy!

I know it is important but really!"

ARI flopped onto the nearest cloud and sighed, resting on the pillow created by the friendly bed.

"So now I must find examples of the spirit of cooperation on a NET adventure to earth.

I also need to have some fun so, let's see. Oh, let's sea – what a good place to start.

I remember that one bird with a yellow head and neck who lived with other seabirds on a cliff. I will fly and find them. They were beautiful- black tips on white wings, light blue bills, and gorgeous head feathers.

Gannets, yes, gannets will be the first stop to check out cooperation among birds. I just love creatures with wings!

What else should I examine for this assignment? Oh, I know. Something else that flies and lives in colonies – bats. They are totally sparkly, flying in the dark for millions of years, cooperating with nature and helping humans too. Bats are great!

One more to go! I remember my classmate Ragu 619 telling the story of bugs marching over the belly of the suit as Ragu watched the sky. That was a funny tale and what were they? Oh, ants! My third example will be ant colonies."

Ari thanked the cloud for the ride and the insights and left for the launchpad.

First stop – St. Kilda, Scotland

"Arrah-arrah," Ari called, mimicking the rasping sound of the gannets. Soon the answer echoed.

"Seabirds are so busy!"

Hundreds of nests tightly packed together.

"That is a cooperating colony if I ever saw one."

Gannets were plunging into the sea for food, sitting on rocks, feeding their young and talking loudly to the neighbors.

"Hello," Ari greeted one parent perching on a pale blue egg. "Pleased to meet you! I am Ari from Angel Academy and would like to learn about cooperation."

"Arrah-arrah," the gannet replied.

So, Ari settled between a few nests and watched quietly.

Movement was endless. Birds flying, diving, bringing food to the young, preening. What a display! Ari enjoyed seeing how well the babies were tended.

"It is amazing that they find their own offspring in this huge grouping. They all look alike to me."

That is part of the lesson. Even though they appear to be the same, to each other they are special. Cooperation honors the similarities and the subtle differences, promotes safety, and encourages good practices by example.

"It sure is noisy but interesting and fun!"

Ari spent the next few hours enjoying the company of gannets.

Evening arrived and Ari decided to seek the next group- bats.

Bats live in caves on six continents so they should be easy to spot.

I hope to see bat "pups" too. Babies are cute in any species!

A group that has occupied space on earth for millions of years must know about cooperation. Since bats eat insects, it would make sense to go to the warmer places where the food supply is greatest. Eating is an important consideration. The gannets stay close to the sea where they can easily fish and the bats are close to the bugs where they feast.

Oh, that is cooperation too. Food sources are a way to find animals. They will follow their food. Interesting!

Overhead Ari spotted bats and followed the stream to the mouth of a cave. Hundreds were emerging. Some were flying so fast they were a blur!

"Bats sure can glide with ease," Ari thought.

Bugs beware! Here they come!

Bats are assistants to farmers because they eat bugs that feast on crops. I know that they also help to pollinate plants and disperse seeds. I wonder if bats know how cooperative they are!

Humans don't always understand the role bats play in the environment and can harm the only mammal capable of true flight.

Harm is the opposite of cooperation. If you are not honored as a true partner, cooperation is not seen as necessary.

I must think about that when I report my findings, Ari noted.

The bats are an enjoyable species to watch so Ari stayed through the night in their company. Bat pups are adorable!

Next stop –

Ants!

I know ants can be found underground, in trees, under rocks and even inside an acorn. Super colonies can have millions and little twigs just a few. They all prefer warmth so that will help in the location.

Ari found a collection near a tree and perched quietly to observe.

Ants certainly know how to cooperate. They are not aggressive with each other but appear hard working and persistent.

I really have no idea what the ants are doing but they seem to communicate with others through touch.

Food is an organizing need even for these tiny creatures. Apart, survival would be impossible, together, ants have thousands of years of history. Life victory is not guaranteed in numbers but is increased through cooperation.

Ants are busy all the time.

Well, that was an interesting NET adventure.

Now to the main ideas for the assignment!

Gannets, bats, and ants are all stellar colony cooperators!

Broods that live together and learn to treat one another non-aggressively can survive for thousands of years.

Social structures develop for the overall good of the colony, but individuals can communicate their own needs through touch, smell, and sound.

Colony decline may occur when another species does not take the time to understand the balance needed for everyone to exist.

Observation is a great method for studying colonies and cooperation.

Harm is the opposite of cooperation.

Ari listened to the low coos of the doves in the tree nearby and realized-

*fear diminishes cooperation and can break apart connections.

*moments of grace-filled communication can save struggle.

*uniqueness and purpose can be felt deeply even if it cannot be observed readily by outsiders.

*victory for a species is not guaranteed but is enhanced by cooperation no matter the level of individual contribution.

The steady cooing of the doves was a touching conclusion to noting how unlike creatures can interact fondly.

Ari smiled and rushed back to Angel Academy to share this latest adventure. Ari's wristlet added charms to complete the journey – a tiny blue gannet egg, a free-tailed bat pup and a colony ant.

ARI 419, upon graduation from Angel Academy, will become

ARIEL, the archangel who loves the environment and its creatures. EL is added to the end of young angel's names to signify that they work for the creator. EL means "of God." Archangel Ariel is known as the lioness of God. She is a fierce defender of earth. Ariel plants the desire to care about the environment in the minds and hearts of humans who work to improve earth cooperation.

ABOUT THE AUTHOR

Joanne Wiess lives in Pennsylvania, USA, with her rescue dog Bristol. Angels have always been a fascinating part of a well-lived life – guiding, nudging, and surprising – leading toward positive outcomes and wonderful people and experiences.